To:

_____

From:

_____

Date:

_____

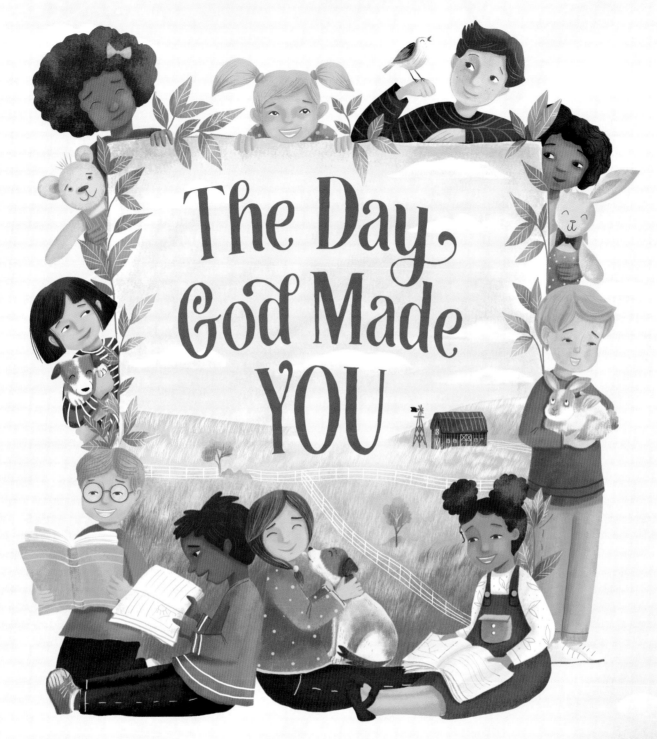

# The Day God Made YOU

BY RORY FEEK

*Illustrated by Malgosia Piatkowska*

An Imprint of Thomas Nelson

*The Day God Made You*

© 2020 Rory Feek

Tommy Nelson, PO Box 141000, Nashville, TN 37214

Published in Nashville, Tennessee, by Tommy Nelson. Tommy Nelson is an imprint of Thomas Nelson. Thomas Nelson is a registered trademark of HarperCollins Christian Publishing, Inc.

Published in association with Atticus Brand Partners, 611 Shenandoah Drive, Brentwood, Tennessee 37027.

Tommy Nelson titles may be purchased in bulk for educational, business, fund-raising, or sales promotional use. For information, please e-mail SpecialMarkets@ ThomasNelson.com.

ISBN 978-1-4002-2353-4 (eBook)

**Library of Congress Control Number: 2020004763**

ISBN 978-1-4002-2350-3

Illustrated by Malgosia Piatkowska

*Printed in the United States of America*

24 25 26   PC   10 9 8 7 6 5 4 3 2

**Mfr: DSC / Shenzhen, China / May 2020 / PO #9547482**

To my little Indiana,

Your mama and I needed you,
And the world needs you too.
God knew all these things
The day He made you.

                 With all my love,
                 Papa

The shape of your eyes,
The color of your hair,
The way that you laugh,
And the size shoes you wear.

The sound of your voice
And the tears you cry too—
God knew all these things
The day He made you.

The way you like puppies
And swinging on swings,
And how ice cream and cookies
Are your favorite things.

How much you love dancing
And trips to the zoo—
God knew all these things
The day He made you.

The family you're part of
And their families before,
The place where you live
And the neighbors next door.

The friends that you have
And the school you go to—
God knew all these things
The day He made you.

The way that you'll grow up,
How tall you'll be,
The job that you'll have,
And the things that you'll see.

The dreams that you'll dream
That one day come true—
God knew all these things
The day He made you.

The life that you'll live,
The things that you'll know,
The adventures you'll take,
And the places you'll go.

The lessons you'll learn
From what you'll go through—
God knew all these things
The day He made you.

The people you'll meet,
The things that you'll do,
The difference you'll make
By just being you.

The love that you give,
The prayers you pray too—
God knew all these things
The day He made you.

Yes, He took the best of your mama
And the best of your dad
And with just the right timing
And all the love that they had . . .

He mixed them together,
And when He was through,
God smiled a big smile
The day He made you!